CHRISTMAS CONFLAGRATION

A TWISTED CHRISTMAS SHORT STORY

ALEXANDRIA BLAELOCK

BlueMere Books
MELBOURNE, AUSTRALIA

For permission requests, please contact
enquiries@bluemerebooks.com.

Ordering Information:
Discounts are available on quantity purchases. For details, contact orders@bluemerebooks.com.

Christmas Conflagration/Alexandria Blaelock
paperback ISBN: 978-1-922744-01-2
digital ISBN: 978-1-922744-02-9

CHRISTMAS CONFLAGRATION

Matilda May McDonald was the crazy cat lady.

The fact that she didn't have any cats didn't seem to matter to the rest of the village.

Nor the fact that she owned four dogs; an Alsatian called Nellie, a Spaniel named Blackie, a Kelpie called Cobber, and a Yorkie named Billie.

Generally, when Matilda saw cats hanging around her place, she let the dogs loose to chase them off.

And when she saw them on the street, she hissed and told them to SCRAM.

But, as far as the village was concerned, the only fact that mattered was that Matilda lived in a ramshackle, half falling down house, with an overgrown garden.

And that she appeared at least 105!

Matilda, known as Tilly to her friends, was actually only 55, but had fully enjoyed her sun-drenched, tiny bikini-clad youth at the beach.

The one she had to take a bus and two trains to get to.

The consequent sun damage was so severe she required biannual dermatology appointments to have the resulting cancers frozen off, which gave her skin an unfortunate scarred and pockmarked appearance due to the blistering.

Though this was much better than the crescent-shaped surgical scar on her face, the trigger for the dermatology appointments in the first place.

And the reason why she didn't care for any further surgeries.

In the main, Tilly preferred "crazy cat lady" to the historical alternative of "witch."

The village was more tolerant of crazy cat ladies than witches, and there were fewer incidents of ringing the doorbell and running away, faecal infernos on the door-mat, and less stone-throwing.

She'd lived alone most of her life; her husband-to-be having got frozen feet and left her at the altar with no explanation or further contact, after which point, she swore off men altogether.

Only rarely did a semi-educated person call her Miss Havisham, and then only once, as Matilda had grown a ruthless streak that didn't allow second chances.

Having lived alone for such a long time, she had developed the habit of talking to herself.

And holding one-sided conversations with the cockatoos, magpies, and possums she shared her garden with.

And the occasional wandering echidna.

Not forgetting the night-time conversations with owls, Australian fruit bats, and foxes.

Who were coincidentally, three-quarters of the way responsible for how overgrown the garden was.

And even Tilly was aware of the irony given people like her are sometimes referred to as fruit bats.

Talking to herself *had* been a problem.

But after watching a couple of episodes of *Continuum*, she started wearing a Bluetooth headset when she was out which at least meant people weren't staring at her.

Well, given the way she generally dressed, not much anyway.

She had a... let's say... distinctive way of dressing.

In her younger days, the late nineties and early oughties, she'd bought a lot of clothes.

Most of them fairly well made, so she'd never seen a need to update her image with more recently fashionable clothes she didn't much like.

Perhaps in America or England someone would've sent her on a makeover show, but not here in Australia.

Tilly particularly loved leopard print, unstructured granny dresses, flannies, boot cut jeans, leggings, and low-cut matching tracksuits.

And to match them; platform heels, Doc Martens and cowboy boots.

For that matter, having mismatched nail art when it wasn't fashionable, or ironic, probably wasn't helping matters either.

Anyone seeing her, and not the professional nail job, would quite rightly think she was either homeless or living in a squat somewhere.

Though to be perfectly honest, she'd inherited the squat house when her parents had ended their lives driving off a long, straight stretch of rural highway into the only tree for miles around while she was away at university.

Her profession was social work, and she worked in the community.

Her shambolic appearance, which to be honest she didn't see anything wrong with, was an excellent way of disarming what many "normal" people would also consider the "crazies."

She was in the habit of bringing said "crazies" into her home; human and animal both.

The four previously mentioned dogs and currently five mismatched, misplaced and misunderstood humans.

The villagers would have been scandalised if they knew, but like any "normal" person, they tended to avert their gaze and not look directly at what was going on at the crazy cat lady's house.

Some of them made gestures to ward off bad luck as they walked by.

Fat lot of good it did them too.

Tilly's property was situated on a large plot of about ten acres of mostly wild eucalypt and fern forest on the outskirts of town, so there wasn't a great deal of casual walking past anyway.

She and her five... house guests had been preparing for Christmas.

Not that any of them were particularly Christmas oriented people who liked a good party with friends and family.

Being more of the kind of people who need quiet time alone as much, if not more than shelter, food and water.

However, they were aware that being seen to not be fully on board with Christmas was a sure-fire way to quench the milk of human kindness of approximately 99.5% of "normal" people.

So they hung decorations, and because Tilly was the only one with a job, prepared handmade gifts crafted from the largess of the land.

Sadly, it takes a special kind of person to appreciate a handmade gift these days. And we're not talking about macaroni necklaces or sad scribbles masquerading as art.

We're talking about actual art; sticks whittled into charming representations of animals, charcoal landscape drawings, and scarves knitted from possum and other furs (including dog and cat) caught in the fencing wires around Tilly's property.

And my personal favourite, a lovingly handcrafted story written by a child of my acquaintance, (I expect it'll be worth something one day).

Is it odd, I wonder, that the most creative people are also the craziest?

Even sadder to my mind, the "crazies" were making a lot of art to sell at the village craft market in the hope of making enough money to purchase something wonderful that Tilly would love.

And to look at it, and know wihout doubt she was loved by others.

Which is ironic, because she *was* that special kind of person who loves handmade art.

Especially the kind that comes from the heart and not through an agent who makes all the money in the exchange.

And perhaps it was that they were all working on their own projects, and not the *really* bad TV reception that meant they were unaware the famous Evangelist Brother Jimmy Marrs would be visiting the village for one night only the week before Christmas.

Had they known, they might have gone because they thought he'd be good for a laugh.

They might even have bathed before arriving.

And had that been the case, they would almost certainly have been doomed.

But as it was, Tilly and her four dogs and five crazy humans slept blissfully through the night. Waking up the next day in a universe that was similar in many ways to their own, but quite different in several key respects.

The main one being that Tilly had lost her crazy cat lady status, and become something far worse than a witch.

She had become the source of all the villages woes; a scapegoat.

Not that any of the villagers would have been able to adequately explain what exactly their woes were.

Only the Jimmy Marrs of this world can do that.

They settled for grumbling about her and the effect she had on the village, (which the day before had been nothing).

Grumbling turned to complaining.

And complaining to carping.

Via envy, through jealousy and onto vicious fault-finding.

Malcontented escalated further to offended and onwards to disaffected.

Like the most virulent of viruses spreading through the community, until nothing would satisfy them but blood.

Within twenty-four hours they had worked themselves into a frenzy.

Coming together at the local church for Carols by Candlelight.

Mrs Van Beek had decorated the church for the annual event with red and green arrangements of Australian natives gathered from local gardens and bushland.

Including southern cypress, woolly bushes, and gum leaves, interspersed with red bottlebrushes, holly-leaved grevilleas and Christmas Bells.

And of course, candles.

The old-fashioned kind you had to light on fire.

Despite there being a Total Fire Ban.

Despite it being a Code Red fire danger day.

She thought they'd be safe because she used tulip shaped wind protectors that also capture the hot was droplets.

It was sweltering that night, so they opened all the doors and windows to let what passed for a breeze into the church.

The breeze that was not even enough to set the candles flickering.

It was a lovely, though not exactly tuneful night.

The high school band played, and the local primary school choir sang.

Local girl made good, opera singer Maggie Moore, sang a couple of songs, encouraging the audience to sing along.

And when it was over, they found the fridge had packed up, but they took their lukewarm beer and wine, with the cheese sweating in the heat into the church garden and ate and drank it anyway.

And of course, that was somehow Tilly's fault as well.

They looked up the hill, and plain as day, there was Tilly's house looking back at them.

All the windows blazing with light, as though she was defiantly not attending church.

Boldly refusing to contribute to the community by buying drinks and raffle tickets.

Challenging the community to do something about it.

One by one, they stood and assembled in a huddle on the lawn looking up.

They were sweltering in the heat.

Befuddled by drink.

Ill with the bad cheese, though they didn't know it yet.

Filled with savage and bitter resentment.

Someone has to do something they agreed.

And then someone did.

Scorned suitor Baz Bell stalked into the church, grabbed a candle and started striding up the hill.

And one by one, the others did the same, until there were no more candles.

Running to fall in behind Baz.

And those without candles were carried away in the rush.

It is a testament to the power of their false bravado that they walked for fifteen minutes uphill until they reached Tilly's place.

They attributed the darkness of the windows to Tilly hiding like the coward they thought she was.

Baz broke stride at the fence, yet forged onward up the long drive. Stopping half or dozen or so paces from the house.

The villagers caught up.

Face working, Baz hurled the candle, protector and all, at the house.

The villagers followed suit shortly after; a barrage of flaming candles.

It had been a fairly dry year, and the house was clad in dusty, leaf and twig decorated spider webs.

They went up like a tinderbox, dropping fiery leaves into the dead garden beds beneath.

Candle flame licked the garden before deciding it liked the taste and consuming it all.

The leaf litter on the ground caught light, smouldering until finally, a hot breeze rose up.

Embers blew around the villagers, setting fire to the twigs, leaves and the shedding bark of the trees.

The villagers were able to swot and stamp out the embers that threatened them, but they couldn't fo anything about those that settled into the leaf stuffed gutters.

Tiny fires set in the small branches, and grew to the larger branches, and before they knew what was happening, the forest exploded in a whirlwind of insects, birds, and small mammals fleeing in all directions.

After a short, stunned pause, Tilly startled them by smashing open the French Doors on the front sitting room.

Four dogs and five humans erupted out of the blazing house.

The villagers abruptly sobered up.

Waking up from the pernicious teachings of Brother Jimmy Marrs.

And less than four and a half minutes after Baz had thrown the first candle, it was already too late.

The flames had engulfed the house, and with the stiffening breeze coming up the hill, pushing the fire ahead of itself, the blaze caught up with the volatile gases from the gum trees; they could see fireballs exploding just above the fire as it raced uphill.

Baz Bell dropped to his knees and howled as he realised what he had done.

You see, Baz was the captain of the local Fire Brigade, and this incident would see him imprisoned for arson.

Worse, for him, barred from the fire fighting forces forever.

Tilly on the other hand laughed.

She laughed until she cried.

She laughed until she couldn't stand up any longer and fell to her knees as well.

She laughed until she couldn't breathe and her breath came in sobbing gasps.

The villagers hustled around her, thinking the poor crazy cat lady was in shock.

They picked her up and carried her away down the driveway.

What the villagers didn't know, was that Tilly laughed because she was free.

Free of the parents who'd cursed her to live a life she hated.

Free of the chains that bound her to her past.

Free to travel, to meet new people, to do whatever she wanted.

That was why she'd never spent any money on the house or land.

She'd wanted it condemned so she could knock it down, even though she wasn't sure that would be enough to end the curse.

But with the house and land razed by the fierceness of the fire, it was enough.

Someone called emergency services, and the wail of sirens and prayers was soon answered by heavy rain.

First, the rain evaporated as it met the flames, and then it steamed as it met the ground, and just as the fire brigade finally arrived with ambulances in tow, it was setting in puddles on the ground.

And when the authorities asked how it started, Tilly said she didn't know.

That the villagers had run up the hill to help.

And the villagers were thankful and found places for herself, her dogs and her humans.

They took up a collection and sent her to a day spa, a hairdresser, and bought her some new fashionable clothes.

And when she came back, they barely recognised her.

It was Baz Bell who asked, "Tilly, is that you?"

And so the villagers forgot the crazy cat lady and she became Tilly once more.

When the insurance money came through, she put it in the bank.

And when the property sold, to a developer of retirement villages, she put the money in the bank.

And when the time came, she packed a small bag and bought a one-way plane ticket out of there.

Though Baz still receives postcards from strange and exotic locations, and he hopes that one day soon, she might come home.

THE END

ABOUT THE AUTHOR

Alexandria Blaelock writes stories, some of them for *Ellery Queen's Mystery Magazine* and *Pulphouse Fiction Magazine*. She's also written five self-help books applying business techniques to personal matters like getting dressed, cleaning house, and feeding your friends.

As a recovering Project Manager, she's probably too fond of sticking to plan. She lives in a forest because she enjoys birdsong, the scent of gum leaves and the sun on her face. When not telecommuting to parallel universes from her Melbourne based imagination, she watches K-dramas, talks to animals, and drinks Campari. At the same time.

Discover more at www.alexandriablaelock.com.

BOOKS BY
ALEXANDRIA BLAELOCK

SHORT STORY COLLECTIONS

The Histories of Hayward Hall
Lovelorn, Lovestruck and Love at First Sight
Common or Garden Variety Heroes
Case Files of the Wilkinson Detective Agency
Unavoidable Fates
Christmas Travesties

OTHER FICTION

That Love Nonsense

MS BLAELOCK'S BOOKS

Stress Free Dinner Parties
Signature Wardrobe Planning
Holistic Personal Finance
Minimally Viable Housekeeping
Planning a Life Worth Living

SELECTED SHORT STORIES

Alma's Grace
Balancing the Book
Carmelita Basingstoke
Fate in Your Hands
Kiss of Death
Lady of the Looking Glass
Life in the Security Directorate
Long Weekend in the Snow
Love in the Past Tense
Love in the Security Directorate
Morning Star, Evening Star, Superstar
Needy Bitch
Payton's Run
Phoenix Child
Secret Singer
Shining Star
Ship in a Bottle
Simone Says Hands in the Air
Special Relativity in Space
The Bygone Boyfriend
The Day the Schedule Broke
The Ghost Detectors
The Guardian's Vigil
The Mince Pie Mystery
The Mystery of the Master Suite
The Pseudonym's Bride
The Shadow Thieves
The Time-Space Paradox
Toy Soldiers

www.ingramcontent.com/pod-product-compliance
Lightning Source LLC
Chambersburg PA
CBHW030815190726
48285CB00003B/1189